# THE HONOR OF HER PEOPLE

BY

JAMES OLIVER CURWOOD

**British Library Cataloguing-in-Publication Data**
A catalogue record for this book is available from the
British Library

# James Oliver Curwood

James Oliver 'Jim' Curwood was an American action-adventure writer and conservationist. He was born on 12th June, 1878, in Owosso, Michigan, USA – as the youngest of four children.

He left high school before graduation, but passed the entrance exam to the University of Michigan, where he enrolled in the English department and studied journalism. After two years, he quit college to become a reporter. In 1900, Curwood sold his first story while working for the Detroit News-Tribune, and after this, his career in writing was made. By 1909 he had saved enough money to travel to the Canadian northwest, a trip that provided the inspiration for his wilderness adventure stories. The success of his novels afforded him the opportunity to return to the Yukon and Alaska for several months each year – allowing Curwood to write more than thirty such books.

By 1922, Curwood's writings had made him a very wealthy man and he fulfilled a childhood fantasy by building 'Curwood Castle' in Owosso. Constructed in the style of an eighteenth century French Chateau, the estate overlooked the Shiawassee River, and made for a truly picturesque setting. In one of the homes' two large turrets, Curwood set up his writing studio. He also owned a camp in a remote area in Baraga County, Michigan, near the Huron Mountains as well as a cabin in Roscommon, Michigan.

Curwood's adventure writing followed in the tradition of Jack London. Like London, Curwood set many of his works in the wilds of the Great Northwest and often used animals as lead characters (Kazan, Baree; Son of Kazan, The Grizzly King and Nomads of the North). Many of Curwood's adventure novels also feature romance as primary or secondary plot consideration. This approach gave his work broad commercial appeal and helped drive his appearance on several best-seller lists in the early 1920s. His most successful work was his 1920 novel, The River's End. The book sold more than 100,000 copies and was the fourth best-selling title of the year in the United States, according to Publisher's Weekly. He contributed to various literary and popular magazines throughout his career, and his bibliography includes more than 200 such articles, short stories and serializations.

Curwood was an avid hunter in his youth; however, as he grew older, he became an advocate of environmentalism and was appointed to the 'Michigan Conservation Commission' in 1926. The change in his attitude toward wildlife can be best expressed by a quote he gave in The Grizzly King: that 'The greatest thrill is not to kill but to let live.' Despite this change in attitude, Curwood did not have an ultimately fruitful relationship with nature. In 1927, while on a fishing trip in Florida, Curwood was bitten on the thigh by what was believed to have been a spider and he had an immediate allergic reaction. Health problems related to the bite escalated over the next few months as an infection set in. He died soon after in his nearby home on Williams Street, on 13th August 1927. He was aged just forty-nine, and was interred in Oak Hill Cemetery (Owosso), in a family plot.

Curwood's legacy lives on however, and his home of Curwood Castle is now a museum. During the first full weekend in June of each year, the city of Owosso holds the Curwood Festival to celebrate the city's heritage, and in addition, a mountain in L'Anse Township, Michigan was given the name Mount Curwood, and the L'Anse Township Park was renamed Curwood Park.

# THE HONOR OF HER PEOPLE

"It ees not so much—What you call heem?—leegend, thees honor of the Beeg Snows!" said Jan softly.

He had risen to his feet and gazed placidly over the crackling box-stove into the eyes of the red-faced Englishman.

"Leegend is lie! Thees is truth!"

There was no lack of luster in the black eyes that roved inquiringly from the Englishman's bantering grin to the others in the room. Mukee, the half Cree, was sitting with his elbows on his knees gazing with stoic countenance at this new curiosity who had wandered four hundred miles northward from civilization. Williams, the Hudson's Bay man who claimed to be all white, was staring hard at the red side of the stove, and the factor's son looked silently at Jan. He and the half-breed noted the warm glow in the eyes that rested casually upon the Englishman.

"It ees truth—thees honor of the Beeg Snows!" said Jan again, and his moccasined feet fell in heavy, thumping tread to the door.

That was the first time he had spoken that evening, and not even the half Cree, or Williams, or the factor's son guessed how the blood was racing through his veins. Outside he stood with the pale, cold glow of the Aurora Borealis shining upon him, and the limitless wilderness, heavy in its burden of snow, reaching out into the ghost-gray fabric of the night. The Englishman's laugh followed him, boisterous and grossly thick, and Jan moved on,—wondering how much longer the half Cree and Williams and the factor's son would listen to the things that this man was saying of the most beautiful thing that had ever come into their lives.

"It ees truth, I swear, by dam'—thees honor of what he calls the 'Beeg Snows!'" persisted Jan to himself, and he set his back to the factor's office and trudged through the snow.

When he came to the black ledge of the spruce and balsam forest he stopped and looked back. It was an hour past bedtime at the post. The Company's store loomed up silent and lightless. The few log cabins betrayed no signs of life. Only in the factor's office, which was the Company's haven for the men of the wilderness, was there a waste of kerosene, and that was because of the Englishman whom Jan was beginning to hate. He stared back at the one glowing window with a queer thickening in his throat and a clenching of the hands in the pockets of his caribou-skin coat. Then he looked long and wistfully at a little cabin which stood apart from the rest, and to himself he whispered again what he had said to the Englishman. Until to-night—or, perhaps, until two weeks ago—Jan had been satisfied with his world. It was a big, passionless world, mostly of snow and ice and endless privation, but he loved it, and there was only a fast-fading memory of another world in his brain. It was a world of big, honest hearts kept warm within caribou skins, of moccasined men whom endless solitude had taught to say little and do much—a world of "Big Snows," as the Englishman had said, in which Jan and all his people had come very close to the things which God created. Without the steely gray flash of those mystery-lights over the Arctic pole Jan would have been homesick; his soul would have withered and died in anything but this wondrous land which he knew, with its billion dazzling stars by night and its eye-blinding brilliancy by day. For Jan, in a way, was fortunate. He had in him an infinitesimal measure of the Cree, which made him understand what the winds sometimes whispered in the pine-tops; and a part of him was French, which added jet to his eyes and a twist to his tongue and made him susceptible to the beautiful, and the rest was "just white"—the part of him that could be stirred into such thoughts and visions as he was now thinking and dreaming of the Englishman.

The "honor of the Beeg Snows" was a part of Jan's soul; it was his religion, and the religion of those few others who lived with him four hundred miles from a settlement, in a place where God's name could not be spelled or written. It meant what civilization could not understand, and the Englishman could not understand—freezing and slow starvation rather than theft, and the living of the tenth

7

commandment above all other things. It came naturally and easily, this "honor of the Beeg Snows." It was an unwritten law which no man cared or dared to break, and to Jan, with his Cree and his French and his "just white" blood, it was in full measure just what the good God meant it to be.

He moved now toward the little isolated cabin, half hidden in its drift of snow, keeping well in the deep shadows of the spruce and balsam, and when he stopped again he saw faintly a gleam of light falling in a wan streak through a big hole in a curtained window. Each night, always when the twenty-odd souls of the post were deep in slumber, Jan's heart would come near to bursting with joy at the sight of this grow from the snow-smothered cabin, for it told him that the most beautiful thing in the world was safe and well. He heard, suddenly, the slamming of a door, and the young Englishman's whistle sounded shrill and untuneful as he went to his room in the factor's house. For a moment Jan straightened himself rigidly, and there was a strange tenseness in the thin, dark face that he turned straight up to where the Northern Lights were shivering in their midnight play. When he looked again at the light in the little cabin the passion-blood was rushing through his veins, and he fingered the hilt of the hunting knife in his belt.

The most beautiful thing in the world had come into Jan's life, and the other lives at the post, just two summers before. Cummins, red-headed, lithe as a cat, big-souled as the eternal mountain of the Crees and the best of the Company's hunters, had brought her up as his bride. Seventeen rough hearts had welcomed them. They had assembled about that little cabin in which the light was shining, speechless in their adoration of this woman who had come among them, their caps in their hands, faces shining, eyes shifting before the glorious ones that looked at them and smiled at them as the woman shook their hands, one by one. Perhaps she was not beautiful, as most people judge. But she was beautiful here—four hundred miles beyond civilization. Mukee, the half-Cree, had never seen a white woman, for even the factor's wife was part Chippewayan, and no one of the others went down to the edge of the southern wilderness more than once each twelve-month or so. Her hair was brown and soft, and it shone with a sunny glory that reached away back into their conception of things dreamed of but never seen, her eyes were as blue as the early snowflowers that came after the spring floods, and her voice was the sweetest sound that had ever fallen upon their ears. So these men thought when Cummins first brought home his wife, and the masterpiece which each had painted in his soul and brain was never changed. Each week and month added to the deep-toned value of that picture, as the passing of a century might add to a Raphael or a Van Dyke. The woman became more human, and less an angel, of course, but that only made her more real, and allowed them to become acquainted with her, to talk with her, and to love her more. There was no thought of wrong—until the Englishman came; for the devotion of these men who lived alone, and mostly wifeless, was a great passionless love unhinting of sin, and Cummins and his wife accepted it, and added to it when they could, and were the happiest pair in all that vast Northland.

The first year brought great changes. The girl—she was scarce more than budding into womanhood—fell happily into the ways of her new life. She did nothing that was elementally unusual—nothing more than any pure woman reared in the love of a God and home would have done. In her spare hours she began to teach the half dozen wild little children about the post, and every Sunday told them wonderful stories out of the Bible. She ministered to the sick, for that was a part of her code of life. Everywhere she carried her glad smile, her cheery greeting, her wistful earnestness to brighten what seemed to her the sad and lonely lives of these silent, worshipful men of the North. And she succeeded, not because she was unlike other millions of her kind, but because of the difference between the fortieth and the sixtieth degrees—the difference in the viewpoint of men who fought themselves into moral shreds in the big game of life and those who lived a thousand miles nearer to the dome of the earth. At the end of this first year came the wonderful event in the history of the Company's post, which had the Barren

Lands at its back door. One day a new life was born into the little cabin of Cummins and his wife.

After this the silent, wordless worship of Jan and his people was filled with something very near to pathos. Cummins' wife was a mother. She was one of them now, a part of their indissoluble existence—a part of it as truly as the strange lights forever hovering over the Pole, as surely as the countless stars that never left the night skies, as surely as the endless forests and the deep snows! There was an added value to Cummins now. If there was a long and dangerous mission to perform it was somehow arranged so that he was left behind. Only Jan and one or two others knew why his traps made the best catch of fur, for more than once he had slipped a mink of an ermine or a fox into one of Cummins' traps, knowing that it would mean a luxury or two for the woman and the baby. And when Cummins left the post, sometimes for a day and sometimes longer, the mother and her child fell as a brief heritage to those who remained. The keenest eyes would not have discovered that this was so.

In the second year, with the beginning of trapping, fell the second and third great events. Cummins disappeared. Then came the Englishman. For a time the first of these two overshadowed everything else at the post. Cummins had gone to prospect a new trap-line, and was to sleep out the first night. The second night he was still gone. On the third day came the "Beeg Snow." It began at dawn, thickened as

11

the day went, and continued to thicken until it became that soft, silent deluge of white in which no man dared venture a thousand yards from his door. The Aurora was hidden. There were no stars in the sky at night. Day was weighted with a strange, noiseless gloom. In all that wilderness there was not a creature that moved. Sixty hours later, when visible life was resumed again, the caribou, the wolf and the fox dug themselves up out of six feet of snow, and found the world changed.

It was at the beginning of the "Beeg Snow" that Jan went to the woman's cabin. He tapped upon her door with the timidity of a child, and when she opened it, her great eyes glowing at him in wild questioning, her face white with a terrible fear, there was a chill at his heart which choked back what he had come to say. He walked in dumbly and stood with the snow falling off him in piles, and when Cummins' wife saw neither hope nor foreboding in his dark, set face she buried her face in her arms upon the little table and sobbed softly in her despair. Jan strove to speak, but the Cree in him drove back what was French and "just white," and he stood in mute, trembling torture. "Ah, the Great God!" his soul was crying. "What can I do?"

Upon its little cot the woman's child was asleep. Beside the stove there were a few sticks of wood. He stretched himself until his neck creaked to see if there was water in the barrel near the door. Then he looked again at the bowed head and the shivering form at the table. In that moment Jan's resolution soared very near to the terrible.

"Mees Cummin, I go hunt for heem!" he cried. "I go hunt for heem—an' fin' heem!"

He waited another moment, and then backed softly toward the door.

"I hunt for heem!" he repeated, fearing that she had not heard.

She lifted her face, and the beating of Jan's heart sounded to him like the distant thrumming of partridge wings. Ah, the Great God—would he ever forget that look! She was coming to him, a new glory in her eyes, her arms reaching out, her lips parted! Jan knew how the Great Spirit had once appeared to Mukee, the half-Cree, and how a white mist, like a snow veil, had come between the half-breed's eyes and the wondrous thing he beheld. And that same snow veil drifted between Jan and the woman. Like in a vision he saw her glorious face so near to him that his blood was frightened into a strange, wonderful sensation that it had never known before. He felt the touch of her sweet breath, he heard her passionate prayer, he knew that one of his rough hands was clasped in both her own—and he knew, too, that their soft, thrilling warmth would remain with him until he died, and still go into Paradise with him.

When he trudged back into the snow, knee-deep now, he sought Mukee, the half-breed. Mukee had suffered a lynx

13

bite that went deep into the bone, and Cummins' wife had saved his hand. After that the savage in him was enslaved to her like an invisible spirit, and when Jan slipped on his snowshoes to set out into the deadly chaos of the "Beeg Storm" Mukee was ready to follow. A trail through the spruce forest led them to the lake across which Jan knew that Cummins had intended to go. Beyond that, a matter of six miles or so, there was a deep and lonely break between two mountainous ridges in which Cummins believed he might find lynx. Indian instinct guided the two across the lake. There they separated, Jan going as nearly as he could guess into the northwest, Mukee trailing swiftly and hopelessly into the south, both inspired in the face of death by the thought of a woman with sunny hair, and with lips and eyes that had sent many a shaft of hope and gladness into their desolate hearts.

It was no great sacrifice for Jan, this struggle with the "Beeg Snows" for the woman's sake. What it was to Mukee, the half-Cree, no man ever guessed or knew, for it was not until the late spring snows had gone that they found what the foxes and the wolves had left of him, far to the south.

A hand, soft and gentle, guided Jan. He felt the warmth of it and the thrill of it, and neither the warmth nor the thrill grew less as the hours passed and the snow fell deeper. His soul was burning with a joy that it had never known. Beautiful visions danced in his brain, and always he heard the woman's voice praying to him in the little cabin, saw her eyes upon him through that white snow veil! Ah, what would he not give if he could find the man, if he could take Cummins back to his wife, and stand for one moment more with her hands clasping his, her joy flooding him with a sweetness that would last for all time! He plunged fearlessly into the white world beyond the lake, his wide snowshoes sinking ankle-deep at every step. There was neither rock nor tree to guide him, for everywhere was the heavy ghost-raiment of the Indian God. The balsams were bending under it, the spruces were breaking into hunchback forms, the whole world was twisted in noiseless torture under its increasing weight, and out through the still terror of it all Jan's voice went in wild echoing shouts. Now and then he fired his rifle, and always he listened long and intently. The echoes came back to him, laughing, taunting, and then each time fell the mirthless silence of the storm. Night came, a little darker than the day, and Jan stopped to build a fire and eat sparingly of his food, and to sleep. It was still night when he aroused himself and stumbled on. Never did he take the weight of his rifle from his right hand or shoulder, for he knew this weight would shorten the distance traveled at each step by his right foot, and would make him go in a circle that would bring him back to the lake. But it was a long circle. The day passed. A second night fell upon him, and his hope of finding Cummins was gone. A chill crept in where his heart had been so warm, and somehow that soft pressure of a woman's hand upon his seemed to become less and less real to him. The woman's prayers were following him, her heart was throbbing with its hope in him—and he had failed! On the third day, when the storm was over, Jan staggered hopelessly into the post. He went straight to the woman, disgraced, heartbroken. When he came out of the little cabin he seemed to have gone mad. A wondrously strange thing had happened. He had spoken not a word, but his failure and his sufferings were written in his face, and when Cummins' wife saw and understood she went as white as the underside of a poplar leaf in a clouded sun. But that was not all. She came to him, and clasped one of his half-frozen hands to her bosom, and he heard her say, "God bless you forever, Jan! You have done the best you could!" The Great God—was that not reward for the risking of a miserable, worthless life such as his? He went to his shack and slept long, and dreamed, sometimes of the woman, and of Cummins and Mukee, the half-Cree.

On the first crust of the new snow came the Englishman up from Fort Churchill, on Hudson's Bay. He came behind six dogs, and was driven by an Indian, and he bore letters to the factor which proclaimed him something of considerable importance at the home office of the Company, in London. As such he was given the best bed in the factor's rude home. On the second day he saw Cummins' wife at the Company's store, and very soon learned the history of Cummins' disappearance.

That was the beginning of the real tragedy at the post. The wilderness is a grim oppressor of life. To those who survive in it the going out of life is but an incident, an irresistible and natural thing, unpleasant but without horror. So it was with the passing of Cummins. But the Englishman brought with him something new, as the woman had brought something new, only in this instance it was an element of life which Jan and his people could not understand, an element which had never found a place, and never could, in the hearts and souls of the post. On the other hand, it promised to be but an incident to the Englishman, a passing adventure in pleasure common to the high and glorious civilization from which he had come. Here again was that difference of viewpoint, the eternity of difference between the middle and the end of the earth. As the days passed, and the crust grew deeper upon the "Beeg Snows," the tragedy progressed rapidly toward finality. At first Jan did not understand. The others did not understand. When the worm of the Englishman's sin revealed itself it struck them with a dumb, terrible fear.

The Englishman came from among women. For months he had been in a torment of desolation. Cummins' wife was to him like a flower suddenly come to relieve the tantalizing barrenness of a desert, and with the wiles and soft speech of his kind he sought to breathe its fragrance. In the weeks that followed the flower seemed to come nearer to him, and this was because Jan and his people had not as yet fully measured the heart of the woman, and because the Englishman had not measured Jan and his people he talked a great deal when enthused by the warmth of the box stove and his thoughts. So human passions were set at play. Because the woman knew nothing of what was said about the box stove she continued in the even course of her pure life, neither resisting nor encouraging the newcomer, yet ever tempting him with that sweetness which she gave to all alike, and still praying in the still hours of night that Cummins would return to her. As yet there was no suspicion in her soul. She accepted the Englishman's friendship. His sympathy for her won him a place in her recognition of things good and true. She did not hear the false note, she saw no step that promised evil. Only Jan and his people saw and understood the one-sided struggle, and shivered at the monstrous evil of it. At least they thought they saw and understood, which was enough. Like so many faithful beasts they were ready to spring, to rend flesh, to tear life out of him who threatened the desecration of all that was good and pure and beautiful to them, and yet, dumb in their devotion and faith, they waited and watched for a sign from the woman. The blue eyes of Cummins' wife, the words of her gentle lips, the touch of her hands had made law at the post. She, herself, had become the omniscience of all that was law to them, and if she smiled upon the Englishman, and talked with him, and was pleased with him, that was only one other law that she had made for them to respect. So they were quiet, evaded the Englishman as much as possible, and watched—always watch ed.

These were days when something worse than disease was eating at the few big honest hearts that made up the life at the post. The search for Cummins never ceased, and always the woman was receiving hope. Now it was Williams who went far into the South, and brought back word that a strange white man had been seen among the Indians; then it was Thoreau, the Frenchman, who skirted the edge of the Barren Lands three days into the West, and said that he had found the signs of strange campfires. And always Jan was on the move, to the South, the North, the East and the West. The days began to lengthen. It was dawn now at eight o'clock instead of nine, the silvery white of the sun was turning day by day more into the glow of fire, and for a few minutes at midday the snow softened and water dripped from the roofs.

Jan knew what it meant. Very soon the thick crust of the "Beeg Snow" would drop in, and they would find Cummins. They would bring what was left of him back to the post. And then—what would happen then?

Every day or two Jan found some pretext that took him to the little log cabin. Now it was to convey to the woman a haunch of a caribou he had slain. Again it was to bring her child a strange plaything from the forest. More frequently it was to do the work that Cummins would have done. He seldom went within the low door, but stood outside, speaking a few words, while Cummins' wife talked to him. But one morning, when the sun was shining down with the first promising warmth of spring, the woman stepped back from the door and asked him in.

"I want to tell you something, Jan," she said softly. "I have been thinking about it for a long time. I must find some work to do. I must do something—to earn—money."

Jan's eyes leaped straight to hers in sudden horror.

"Work!"

The word fell from him as if in its utterance there was something of crime. Then he stood speechless, awed by the look in her eyes, the hard gray pallor that came into her face.

"May God bless you for all you have done, Jan, and may God bless the others! I want you to take that word to them from me. But he will never come back, Jan—never. Tell the men that I love them as brothers, and always shall love them, but now that I know he is dead I can no longer live as a drone among them. I will do anything. I will make your coats, do your washing and mend your moccasins. To-morrow I begin my first work—for money."

He heard what she said after that as if in a dream. When he went out into the day again, with her word to his people, he knew that in some way which he could not understand this big, cold world had changed for him. To-morrow Cummins' wife was to begin writing letters for the Englishman! His eyes glittered, his hands clenched themselves upon his breast, and all the blood in him submerged itself in one wild resistless impulse. An hour later Jan and his four dogs were speeding swiftly into the South.

The next day the Englishman went to the woman's cabin. He did not return in the afternoon. And that same afternoon, when Cummins' wife came into the Company's store, a quick flush shot into her cheeks and the glitter of blue diamonds into her eyes when she saw the Englishman standing there. The man's red face grew redder, and he shifted his gaze. When Cummins' wife passed him she drew her skirt close to her, and there was the poise of a queen in her head, the glory of mother and wife and womanhood, the living, breathing essence of all that was beautiful in Jan's "honor of the Beeg Snows." But Jan, twenty miles to the south, did not know.

He returned on the fourth night and went quietly to his little shack in the edge of the balsam forest. In the glow of the oil lamp which he lighted he rolled up his treasure of winter-caught furs into a small pack. Then he opened his door and walked straight and fearlessly toward the cabin of

21

Cummins' wife. It was a pale, glorious night, and Jan lifted his face to its starry skies and filled his lungs near to bursting with its pure air, and when he was within a few steps of the woman's door he burst into a wild snatch of triumphant forest song. For this was a new Jan who was returning to her, a man who had gone out into the solitudes and fought a great battle with the elementary things in him, and who, because of his triumph over these things, was filled with the strength and courage to live a great lie. The woman heard his voice, and recognized it. The door swung open, wide and brimful of light, and in it stood Cummins' wife, her child hugged close in her arms.

Jan crowed close up out of the starry gloom.

"I fin' heem, Mees Cummins—I fin' heem nint' miles back in Cree wigwam—with broke leg. He come home soon—he sen' great love—an' THESE!"

And he dropped his furs at the woman's feet....

"Ah, the Great God!" cried Jan's tortured soul when it was all over. "At least she shall not work for the dirty Englishman."

First he awoke the factor, and told him what he had done. Then he went to Williams, and after that, one by one, these three visited the four other white and part white men at the post. They lived very near to the earth, these seven, and the spirit of the golden rule was as natural to their living as green sap to the trees. So they stood shoulder to shoulder to Jan in a scheme that appalled them, and in the very first day of this scheme they saw the woman blossoming forth in her old beauty and joy, and at times fleeting visions of the old happiness at the post came to these lonely men who were searing their souls for her. But to Jan one vision came to destroy all others, and as the old light returned to the woman's eyes, the glad smile to her lips, the sweetness of thankfulness and faith into her voice, this vision hurt him until he rolled and tossed in agony at night, and by day his feet were never still. His search for Cummins now had something of madness in it. It was his one hope—where to the other six there was no hope. And one day this spark went out of him. The crust was gone. The snow was settling. Beyond the lake he found the chasm between the two mountains, and, miles of this chasm, robbed to the bones of flesh, he found Cummins. The bones, and Cummins' gun, and all that was left of him, he buried in a crevasse.

He waited until night to return to the post. Only one light was burning when he came out into the clearing, and that was the light in the woman's cabin. In the edge of the balsams he sat down to watch it, as he had watched it a hundred nights before. Suddenly something came between him and the light. Against the cabin he saw the shadow of a human form, and as silently as the steely flash of the Aurora over his head, as swiftly as a lean deer, he sped through the gloom of the forest's edge and came up behind the home of the woman and her child. With the caution of a lynx, his head close to the snow, he peered around the end of the logs. It was the Englishman who stood looking through the tear in the curtained window! Jan's moccasined feet made no sound. His hand fell as gently as a child's upon the Englishman's arm.

"Thees is not the honor of the Beeg Snows!" he whispered. "Come."

A sickly pallor filled the Englishman's face. But Jan's voice was soft and dispassionate, his touch was velvety in its hint, and he went with the guiding hand away from the curtained window, smiling in a companionable way. Jan's teeth gleamed back. The Englishman chuckled. Then Jan's hands changed. They flew to the thick reddening throat of the man from civilization, and without a sound the two sank together upon the snow. It was many minutes before Jan rose to his feet. The next day Williams set out for Fort Churchill with word for the Company's home office that the Englishman had died in the "Beeg Snow," which was true.

The end was not far away now. Jan was expecting it day by day, hour by hour. But it came in a way that he did not expect. A month had gone, and Cummins had not come up from among the Crees. At times there was a strange light in the woman's eyes as she questioned the men at the post. Then, one day, the factor's son told Jan that she wanted to see him in the little cabin at the other end of the clearing.

A shiver went through him as he came to the door. It was more than a spirit of unrest in Jan to-day, more than suspicion, more than his old dread of that final moment of the tragedy he was playing, which would condemn him to everlasting perdition in the woman's eyes. It was pain, poignant, terrible—something which he could not name, something upon which he could place his hand, and yet which filled him with a desire to throw himself upon his face in the snow and sob out his grief as he had seen the little children do. It was not dread, but the torment of reality, that gripped him now, and when he faced the woman he knew why. There had come a terrible change, but a quiet change, in Cummins' wife. The luster had gone from her eyes. There was a dead whiteness in her face that went to the roots of her shimmering hair, and as she spoke to Jan she clutched one hand upon her bosom, which rose and fell as Jan had seen the breast of a mother lynx rise and fall in the last torture of its death.

"Jan," she panted, "Jan—you have lied to me!"

Jan's head dropped. The worn caribou skin of his coat crumpled upon his breast. His heart died. And yet he found voice, soft, low, simple.

"Yes, me lie!"

"You—you lied to me!"

"Yes—me—lie—"

His head dropped lower. He heard the sobbing breath of the woman, and gently his arm crooked itself, and his fingers rose slowly, very slowly, toward the hilt of his hunting knife.

"Yes—Mees Cummins—me lie—"

There came a sudden swift, sobbing movement, and the woman was at Jan's feet, clasping his hand to her bosom as she had clasped it once before when he had gone out to face death for her. But this time the snow veil was very thick before Jan's eyes, and he did not see her face. Only he heard.

"Bless you, dear Jan, and may God bless you evermore! For you have been good to me, Jan—so good—to me—"

And he went out into the day again a few moments later, leaving her alone in her great grief, for Jan was a man in the wild and mannerless ways of a savage world, and he knew not how to comfort in the fashion of that other world which had other conceptions and another understanding of what was to him the "honor of the Beeg Snows." A week later the woman announced her intention of returning to her people, for the dome of the earth had grown sad and lonely and desolate to her now that Cummins was forever gone. Sometimes the death of a beloved friend brings with it the sadness that spread like a pall over Jan and those others who had lived very near to contentment and happiness for nearly two years, only each knew that this grief of his would be as enduring as life itself. For a brief space the sweetest of all God's things had come among them, a pure woman who brought with her the gentleness and beauty and hallowed thoughts of civilization in place of its iniquities, and the pictures in their hearts were imperishable.

The parting was as simple and as quiet as when the woman had come. They went to the little cabin where the sledge dogs stood harnessed. Hatless, silent, crowding back their grief behind grim and lonely countenances, they waited for Cummins' wife to say good-bye. The woman did not speak. She held up her child for each man to kiss, and the baby babbled meaningless things into the bearded faces that it had come to know and love, and when it came to Williams' turn he whispered, "Be a good baby, be a good baby." And when it was all over the woman crushed the child to her breast and dropped sobbing upon the sledge, and Jan cracked his whip and shouted hoarsely to the dogs, for it was Jan who was to drive her to civilization. Long after they had disappeared beyond the clearing those who remained stood looking at the cabin; and then, with a dry, strange sob in his throat, Williams led the way inside. When they came out Williams brought a hammer with him, and nailed the door tight.

"Mebby she'll come back some day," he said.

That was all, but the others understood.

For nine days Jan raced his dogs into the South. On the tenth they came to Le Pas. It was night when they stopped before the little log hotel, and the gloom hid the twitching in Jan's face.

"You will stay here—to-night?" asked the woman.

"Me go back—now," said Jan.

Cummins' wife came very close to him. She did not urge, for she, too, was suffering the torture of this last parting with the "honor of the Beeg Snows." It was not the baby's face that came to Jan's now, but the woman's. He felt the soft touch of her lips, and his soul burst forth in a low, agonized cry.

"The good God bless you, and keep you, and care for you evermore, Jan," she whispered. "Some day we will meet again."

And she kissed him again, and lifted the child to him, and Jan turned his tired dogs back into the grim desolation of the North, where the Aurora was lighting his way feebly, and beckoning to him, and telling him that the old life of centuries and centuries ago was waiting for him there.

www.ingramcontent.com/pod-product-compliance
Lightning Source LLC
Chambersburg PA
CBHW030243180626
46810CB00008B/3269